MW01070937

CINDERELLA AND THE VAMPIRE PRINCE

by Wiley Blevins • illustrated by Steve Cox

RED CHAIR PRESS

Please visit our website at **www.redchairpress.com** for more high-quality products for young readers.

About the Author

Wiley Blevins has taught elementary school in both the United States and South America. He has also written over 70 books for children and 15 for teachers, as well as created reading programs for schools in the U.S. and Asia with Scholastic, Macmillan/McGraw-Hill, Houghton-Mifflin Harcourt, and other publishers. Wiley currently lives and writes in New York City.

About the Artist

Steve Cox lives in London, England. He first designed toys and packaging for other people's characters. But he decided to create his own characters and turned full time to illustrating. When he is not drawing books he plays lead guitar in a rock band.

Publisher's Cataloging-In-Publication Data

Blevins, Wiley.
    Cinderella and the Vampire Prince / by Wiley Blevins ; illustrated by Steve Cox.

    pages : illustrations ; cm. -- (Scary tales retold)

    Summary: "You may know the story of the downtrodden girl who meets her Prince Charming. But our Cinder-Ella rules the dark night with her new Prince."--Provided by publisher.
    Issued also as an ebook.
    ISBN: 978-1-63440-090-9 (library hardcover)
    ISBN: 978-1-63440-091-6 (paperback)

    1. Cinderella (Legendary character)--Juvenile fiction. 2. Vampires--Juvenile fiction. 3. Princes--Juvenile fiction. 4. Cinderella (Legendary character)--Fiction. 5. Vampires--Fiction. 6. Princes--Fiction. 7. Fairy tales. 8. Horror tales. I. Cox, Steve, 1961- II. Title. III. Title: Based on (work) Cinderella.

PZ7.B618652 Ci 2016
[E]   2015940011

Copyright © 2017 Red Chair Press LLC
RED CHAIR PRESS, the RED CHAIR and associated logos are registered trademarks of Red Chair Press LLC.

All rights reserved. No part of this book may be reproduced, stored in an information or retrieval system, or transmitted in any form by any means, electronic, mechanical including photocopying, recording, or otherwise without the prior written permission from the Publisher. For permissions, contact info@redchairpress.com

Scary Tales Retold first published by:
Red Chair Press LLC   PO Box 333   South Egremont, MA 01258-0333

Printed in the United States of America
Distributed in the U.S. by Lerner Publisher Services. www.lernerbooks.com

0516 1 CBGF16

It was a dark and stormy night. At least that's how most scary stories start.

And this is one of the scariest.

Deep in a forest lived a girl named Ella.
Each night she would rub cinders, or ashes from
her fireplace, on her arms and legs to hide in
the dark. Then she would sneak out
for adventure.

People began calling the girl Cinder-Ella.
They would spot her in the night.
Climbing trees. Shouting at the moon.
And playing with forest animals.

During the day, Cinder-Ella lived with her evil stepmother, and two mean and overly clean stepsisters.

Cinder-Ella longed for the day she could leave. She only felt happy when it was dark. But nobody understood her love of the night.

One day a golden envelope was slipped under
her door. It contained an invitation to a ball at a
nearby castle. The prince was looking for a princess.

Cinder-Ella had never wanted to marry a prince.
But she so wanted to escape her mean stepmother
and stepsisters. So she thought, "Hmm . . . maybe
I should go?"

But there was a problem. Unlike her stepsisters, Cinder-Ella had nothing to wear to a prince's ball. And unlike her stepsisters, she had no way to get there. Cinder-Ella sat in a tree and felt sorry for herself.

Just then Cinder-Ella's fairy godfather appeared.
Her sweet and gentle fairy godmother was
away on vacation. It had been a stressful year
watching over Cinder-Ella. Her fairy godfather
was not so kind or trustworthy.

"What will I wear?" asked Cinder-Ella.

Her fairy godfather waved his magic wand
and laughed. Cinder-Ella looked down. She
was wearing a puffy dress with shiny red
designs all over it. Her black sneakers stuck
out from underneath.

"And how will I get to the ball?" asked Cinder-Ella.

"Instead of a pumpkin, I will use this blood-red tomato," laughed her fairy godfather. "The prince will love it!"

The night of the ball arrived.

Cinder-Ella climbed out her bedroom
window and hopped into the tomato carriage.

When she arrived at the prince's castle, everyone stared.

Especially the prince.

"Who is this beautiful girl," whispered the guests—ghosts, mummies, zombies, ghouls, and all sorts of spooky creatures.

"What great costumes," thought Cinder-Ella. But these weren't costumes.

A band of witches began to play music.
The prince strutted over to Cinder-Ella and
asked for the first dance. They twirled and
spun and waltzed around the dance floor.

"Thank you," said the prince. Then he danced with Cinder-Ella's stepsisters and the other girls. The hands of the clock raced around in dizzying speed until it was almost midnight.

"It is time," announced the prince. "I must choose my princess."

The prince carefully took one last sniff of each girl. The stepsisters smelled like roses. Other girls smelled like cinnamon and apple pie. Then he sniffed Cinder-Ella.

"I pick you," he said. "My nose never lies. You will have the tastiest blood."

Cinder-Ella shrieked, "He's a vampire!"
And she bolted out of the castle as the
clock stopped on midnight. One of her black
sneakers fell off on the steep castle stairs.

The prince grabbed her sneaker and chased
after her. "That blood," he yelled. "That
delicious, juicy blood. Please don't leave me.
I will make you my princess of the night."

Cinder-Ella stopped in her tracks.
"Princess of the night . . . ?" Just then
Cinder-Ella realized a vampire prince might
not be so bad after all.

So she married him.

And the two ruled the night . . .
happily ever after.

THE END